GW00739106

School Handbook

FOR

Girls

Lisa Regan

BARDFIELD
PRESS

My Photo

My personal details

This book belongs to...

Kate Bruce

Address: 15A Boodle cresent Sidley

Telephone: 01424 734836 Mobile: 07

Email:

Date of birth: 19,11,95

These are a few...
...of my favourite things

Singers
Gwen stafani, Fergi,

Bands
Take that ,

School subjects
Arts Swimming,
Literacy

Actors/Actresses
Will smith
Billie Piper

Films
Pirates 3
Shrek 3
Simpsons movie
Racing Stripes
Dreamer

Teams
chelsea,
Liverpool

Sports
Horse riding,
running

Hobbies
Horse riding
Running ,
Swimming,
Reading

TV programmes
Simpsons, B brother,
comp shows

Books
Heartland, C,H
Jess the
Border Colie

Birthdays

January
Lillys birthday 6th

February
Mandys birthday 11th

March
Moms birthday 31st

April

May

June
Douglas birthday 27th

July

August
Dads birthday 24th

September
Vincents birthday 28th

October

November
My birthday 19th
Christine birthday 29th
Dinas birthday 21st

December
Hallys birthday 27th
Jakes birthday 4th

Do you need to chill out?

Are you a thrill seeker or a chill merchant?
Follow the boxes to see what
the verdict is below.

START HERE

What's your fave thing to do on a Saturday?

SHOP

What do your shopping trips usually involve?

CAKE IN THE CAFE

SHOP 'TIL YOU DROP

ARRANGING A LIFT

What do you use your mobile for the most?

SPORT

WATCHING

Which do you prefer, then?

PLAYING

When do you do your homework?

AS SOON AS IT'S SET

LAST MINUTE

SLEEPOVER

OVERHEARING BITCHY COMMENTS

What's your ideal night out?

What's more likely to stress you out?

CINEMA

MISSING THE BUS

LAST TO LEAVE

TEXTING A FRIEND

FIRST OUT OF THE DOOR

At the end of school, are you...?

What's your fave fairground ride?

CAT

CAROUSEL

DODGEMS

What's your favourite animal?

DOG

WATCHING TV

How do you relax?

PLAYING COMPUTER GAMES

FROSTY

Hey there, frosty! No – you're not a cold-hearted person, but you're so chilled out you'd feel at home in the Arctic! It's great news that you're living such a lovely life, but have you ever thought that if you stepped things up a notch, you could fit even more fun into your time?

BALANCED

The only way to improve on a good thing is to keep an eye on any friends who are too fast or too furious – teach them to take time out, too. Balance is the name of your game – you're happy to race around when things need to be done, but you're equally good at taking time out when it all gets too much.

WOAH!

Woah, there! It's surprising you even found time to finish this quiz – is there anything you don't do at breakneck speed? Life in the fast lane has its thrills, for sure, but don't forget that as you speed through life, you're going to miss out sometimes. Don't let the good things pass you by.

HOW GREEN ARE YOU?

Test your knowledge and your habits to see if you're saving the world or wrecking your future.

1 Which of these kinds of cans can be recycled?

A Aluminium

B Steel

C Both aluminium and steel ✓

2 Recycling a single can saves roughly how much electricity?

A Enough to power your TV for 30 minutes

B Enough to power your TV for one-and-a-half hours

C Enough to power your TV for three hours ✓

3 Which of these can be used to clean your sink?

A Butter

B Mineral water

C Flat coke ✓

4 Which of these do you recycle at home?

A Glass and newspapers

B Cans, glass, paper and card

C Plastic, cans, glass, paper, card, old clothes and shoes ✓

5 Where is our household rubbish disposed of?

A It's taken to the rubbish dump and burned

B It's taken to the sea and thrown away

C It's buried in a hole called a landfill site ✓

6 Which of these is a good use for newspaper (before you recycle it, of course)?

A Cleaning your hands

B Cleaning dusty surfaces

C Cleaning windows ✓

7 Why is it important to recycle paper?

A To save trees

B To save energy

C To save energy, trees and the wildlife that lives in the trees ✓

8 Which of these do you persuade your family to do?

A Only shop at places that provide posh carrier bags

B Only use the free carrier bags provided at supermarkets

C Take along your own shopping bags and reuse the carriers from the supermarket ✓

9 What's the worst option of the three below?

A Leaving the fridge door open for a minute

B Leaving the room door ajar when the heating is on

C Leaving the TV on standby overnight ✓

10 Which of these should you always do to benefit the environment?

A Flush the toilet every time you use it

B Wash your face in cold water instead of using the warm tap

C Turn off a running tap whilst you're brushing your teeth ✓

How did you score?

Did you score mostly **A** , **B** or **C** ? Well, here's hoping it was **C** because they're the only correct answers all the way through! Read back to see what you can be doing and what you need to know to help save the world's resources. It's your world and you live in it, so it's up to you to help out as much as you can. Ignorance is not bliss in this instance!

Diplomat
or
DINGBAT?

START

Do people often ask you for advice?

NO → **Are you happy in a small group?**

NO

YES

YES → **Do you sometimes wish you could take back your last statement?**

Do you prefer animals to people?

YES

YES

NO

NO

Do you often blush when you've finished talking?

YES

NO

Do you admire people who are good with words?

NO

Do you prefer to complain in writing rather than face to face?

YES

YES

NO

Do you always say the right thing, or do you constantly cringe because you've put your foot in it? Do this fun quiz to find out where you are on the blushometer. If you're near the top, it might be time to start thinking before you speak. If you're near the bottom, maybe you should consider a career in the diplomatic service?!

CRINGE

BLUSHOMETER

Are you good at maths?

NO

Do you struggle to think of the right word?

YES

YES

NO

NO

Do you read a lot?

YES

Do you think rappers are clever with words?

NO

YES

YES

Are there only a couple of friends you confide in?

Do you constantly worry that you've said the wrong thing?

NO

YES

NO

NO

Do you think things through before discussing them with others?

YES

Do you think politicians are clever with the truth?

NO

YES

PHEW!

Dream Jeans

Jeans are a must-have item in everyone's wardrobe, but how do you choose the perfect pair? It all depends on your body shape – read on for some trade secrets!

Rear of the year

If you're concerned that your bottom is too big to wear jeans, think again. Choose a pair with large rear pockets to minimize your bum. Small pockets make it look bigger and no pockets will make it look huuuuuuuge!

Too tall!

Do you struggle to buy jeans that reach the floor? Check out specialist tall sections of some high-street stores, or make the most of your height and wear cropped jeans and cute ballet pumps. (Shorties should avoid cropped trousers, so tall girls just got lucky!)

Tomboy time

If you have the figure of a schoolboy, with no bottom or curves, sing with joy! You're the only person who should be buying jeans with flap pockets. Look out, too, for jeans with curved waistbands and lots of detail such as rips and fancy seams.

Beat the bulge

If you feel that jeans are unflattering to your flabby bits, panic not. Stick to wide leg jeans (skinnies are a no-no) and don't be tempted to buy a size too small as they'll show off your worst bits. Dark colours and heavy denim are a good disguise-idea, too.

Pear-shaped

Draw attention away from your thigh area with fancy hems or bright-coloured tops. Stick to very dark jeans to slim you down and wear boots with heels to make you seem taller and slimmer. Avoid extra pockets on the front or sides of your jeans.

Tiny tots

Small girls can look great in jeans, but not if they're too big or flared. If you're short, choose jeans with a crease or line (such as a pin-tuck) down the leg to make your legs look longer.

FOODY FACTS

How much do you know about the way you're fuelling your body? Here are just a few fab facts.

Strawberries

As well as counting towards your five-a-day target, strawberries contain fibre and Vitamin C. In fact, weight for weight, they have more Vitamin C than oranges.

Ginger

If you get travel sick, try nibbling on ginger biscuits. Ginger is a natural way to beat nausea.

Milk

Some scientists believe that drinking organic milk can help your body fight off colds and flu more effectively than if you drink non-organic milk.

Cakes

Eating too many cakes and biscuits isn't good for you. Although tasty, they're packed with sugar and fat – and should only be eaten as an occasional snack!

Cheese

Cheese provides calcium, protein, minerals and vitamins. Higher-fat cheeses also provide CLA, which lowers cholesterol and boosts your immune system.

Pasta

If you're feeling stressed, eat pasta! The starchiness helps your brain produce a chemical called serotonin, which makes you feel happier.

Apples

Recent research has shown that eating an apple a day can help reduce the risk of asthma and improve your lungs.

Cola

As well as being sugary, cola also contains high levels of phosphorous. This interferes with your body's absorption of calcium, so is bad for your bones.

Kiwis

Kiwi fruits are one of the best easily available sources of Vitamin C.

Nuts

A tooth-friendly snack, nuts contain virtually no carbohydrates and don't cause tooth decay! They're also packed with minerals, fibre and vitamins.

Feel-good factor

Are you feeling low? Do you struggle to get out of bed in the morning? Are you too stressed to think straight? Try these quick fixes for an instant boost.

Sniff an apple!

The smell of apples has a calming effect, so slice one into pieces and have a good sniff. Then eat it and contribute to your five-a-day target.

Give someone a cuddle

Go on – grab a friend and give them a good squeeze. It's good for them and will give you a surge of feel-good hormones.

Boogie on down!

Put on your fave CD and bop 'til you drop. Not only will the exercise make you feel fab, but singing along to your fave tune will always make you smile!

Relax!

Kneel on all fours and then move your bottom onto your heels. Slide your arms out straight in front of you until your forehead is on the ground. Breathe deeply feeling the air move in your chest. And relax!

Scream!

Open your mouth and start to scream – silently. Force the air out without making any noise. It helps relax your face muscles and calm your body.

Eat a banana

They're full of energy-boosting chemicals to make you feel happier and less stressed.

Grab some rays

If it's a sunny day, walk in the sunshine to boost your serotonin levels – the chemical that makes you feel good.

Energy boost

Rub your palms quickly up and down the outside of your shins, just to the side of your shinbone. Do it 18 times to give you extra energy and boost your immune system.

Think positively!

Sit in front of your mirror each morning and think about something good in your life. It might be small or large, such as "I just got amazing exam results" or "Great, my horrible spot has gone". There's always something to feel good about, even if it's "I can't wait to wear my new earrings"!

Raid the KITCHEN

...not because you've got the munchies, but to find some excellent ingredients for do-it-yourself beauty treatments.

Please remember, different people have different reactions to ingredients. Always test first on a small patch of skin, for example, inside the lower arm or just below your jaw. Do not use if you have broken skin or are allergic to any ingredients.

SQUEAKY CLEAN

Make a super-cool cleanser to wash away your worries! Peel a cucumber and either mash it or put it in a food blender. Then put it through a sieve to get rid of the seeds. Mix the cucumber with milk or plain yoghurt, and place in the fridge to chill. Use cotton wool to apply to your skin, avoiding the delicate eye area, and then gently remove.

ZINGY MOUTHWASH

Make your breath smell sweet with this lemon explosion! Squeeze a few drops of lemon into your mouth and swish it round. The citric acid kills bacteria in your mouth, instantly giving you brilliantly fresh breath.

SUPER SOFT

Make a mega-moisturizing face pack using an avocado, one-and-a-half teaspoons of lemon juice, one teaspoon of honey and two teaspoons of plain yoghurt. Mash all the ingredients in a bowl until they form a smooth paste. Chill in the fridge for up to half an hour. Spread onto your face, avoiding the delicate skin around your eyes, and leave for no more than 15 minutes. Rinse thoroughly with lukewarm water.

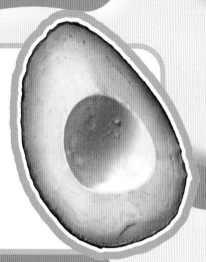

FRUITY FEET

Mash together a handful of strawberries (about eight) with the tops cut off. Mix in two tablespoons of olive oil and three tablespoons of rock salt or sea salt. Massage the mix into your feet, especially on areas with hard skin, and then wash off and moisturize your feet.

HAIR CARE

For super-shiny, stronger hair, use this banana mix every week. Mash one ripe banana in a bowl and mix in three tablespoons of mayonnaise and one-and-a-half tablespoons of olive oil. Smooth over your hair and wrap it in clingfilm fixed with hair clips. Relax for 15 minutes and then rinse off in cool water before using your normal shampoo.

Wish Lists...

Be my Valentine

People you'd like to get a card from

1 Ollie
2
3
4
5

People you'll send a card to

1
2
3
4
5

CHRISTMAS PRESSIES

Presents you would like

1 Horse
2 Cloths
3 funky beanbeg
4 redecorate room
5 skyhd plus

People you need to give to

1 mom + Dad
2 bst buddys
3 foster perents
4 siblings
5 femiy

Changing the world

Ways you'd like to change the world to make it a better place

1 Everyone turns echo friendly
2 there are less bitchy chevs
3 people respect animals + environment
4
5

People you'd love to meet

1. Jonny Dept
2. Billie Piper
3.
4.
5.
6.
7.
8.
9.
10.

Things to do

Places to go
1. Cube - caravian
2. miami
3. New york
4. Veginia
5. Alps - Africa

Activities to do
1. ride a dolphin
2. goon riding holiday
3. go skuba diving
4. get in touch with animal
5.

Future goals

Things you're going to make happen in the coming year

1. Buy more pressies for friends + family
2. Work harder in lessons at school
3. eat less sweets so I loose weit
4. stand up to people and be brave
5.

How to use your diary

If you have a thirst for knowledge, weekly lists and fascinating facts will keep you entertained for hours on end.

Clever clogs

Dolphins are intelligent mammals. They can learn many tricks and stunts, like leaping through hoops, knocking balls with their beaks, and giving people rides on their backs. They can recognize many different shapes, count and mimic sounds.

Bizarre US laws

Alaska – it's illegal to look at a moose through the window of an aeroplane.

Ohio – pets must have lights on their tails at night.

Kentucky – it's illegal to carry an ice-cream cone in your pocket.

Minnesota – dog owners will be fined if their pet chases a cat up a telegraph pole.

Illinois – bees are forbidden from flying over the tow

Oklahoma – it is illegal to get a fish drunk.

Nebraska – barbers may not eat onions between 7 a.m. and 7 p.m.

STICKERS!

 Birthday party

Shopping trip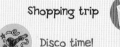

Disco time!

Sporty spell

Fabulous day

Holiday fun

Love life

QUIZ

1 What is the name of Scotland's largest loch?

2 Is the cross on the Norwegian flag red, white or blue?

3 In which US city can the Golden Gate bridge be found?

4 How many oceans are there in the world – two, four or six?

5 Tenerife and Lanzarote belong to which island group?

h Lomond 2 Blue 3 San Francisco
4 5 The Canaries

What's brown and sticky?

A stick

Test how much of a brainbox you really are with these quick quizzes. Then give your brain a break and have a laugh with some hilarious jokes.

Write the month at the top of the page and the dates in the hearts.

September

school notes

fun time

19 Monday

Maths homework due in

Cinema with Rosie 7 p.m.

20 Tuesday

Science project due in

Pick up Anne for netball practice

21 Wednesday

English lesson in library today

 I ♥ Jack!!!!

22 Thursday

School trip to Tower of London

Sleepover at Beth's

23 Friday

it's the weekend

24 Saturday

 Shopping with Jo 11 a.m.

Philippa coming round for tea

25 Sunday

Belinda's birthday party 6 p.m.

You'll never again need to use the excuse, "My dog ate my homework!" With this super diary, you'll be so organized that your school work will always be handed in on time.

Use your stickers to show something special, such as a fabulous day, when you're shopping with friends, or when *that* boy looks your way...!

Whether it's a birthday party, disco or a shopping trip with friends, the last thing you want to do is miss out. Jot down your fun time activities and get your weekend sorted.

Horse tails

Told from the viewpoint of a horse, Anna Sewell's **Black Beauty** (published in 1877) was actually written to teach adults about animal welfare but soon became a children's classic.

Before they were famous

Vic Reeves worked on a pig farm
Jennifer Aniston was a waitress, just like Rachel!
George Michael had a Saturday job at BHS
Madonna worked at Dunkin' Donuts
Michael Douglas started as a petrol pump attendant
Lucy Lui stretched her stuff as an aerobics instructor
Ozzy Osbourne was a slaughterhouse labourer, ugh!
Kate Winslet served sandwiches in a north London deli
Robbie Williams sold double glazing
Brad Pitt delivered fridges

QUIZ

1 Which contestant won the TV contest **The X Factor** in 2005?

2 Who is the voice of Rodney Copperbottom in the 2005 animation, **Robots**?

3 Which film starred Cameron Diaz, Lucy Lui and Drew Barrymore as a crime-fighting trio?

4 For which film did Jamie Foxx win an Oscar® for Best actor in a leading role?

5 Which soap opera is set in Walford?

answers
1 Shayne Ward 2 Ewan McGregor 3 Charlie's Angels 4 Ray 5 Eastenders

What do you call a stupid dinosaur?

A thick-a-saurus

school notes

Monday _____
_____
_____
_____

Tuesday _____
_____
_____
_____

Wednesday _____
_____
_____
_____

Thursday _____
_____
_____
_____

Friday _____
_____
_____

fun time

_____
_____
_____
_____
_____
_____
_____
_____
_____
_____
_____
_____
_____
_____
_____
_____
_____
_____
_____

it's the weekend

Saturday
_____
_____
_____
_____

Sunday
_____
_____
_____
_____

Scorching!

The Sun is about 150 million kilometres from Earth. A spacecraft travelling at the speed of a jet airliner – 900 kilometres an hour – would take about 20 years to reach the Sun.

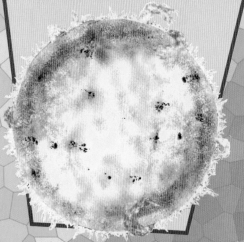

Really wild tunes

Hungry Like the Wolf – Duran Duran
Eye of the Tiger – Survivor
Ape Man – The Kinks
Buffalo Soldier – Bob Marley
Hound Dog – Elvis Presley
I Am the Walrus – The Beatles
Love Cats – The Cure
Monkey Wrench – Foo Fighters
Puppy Love – Donny Osmond
Who Let the Dogs Out – Baha Men

QUIZ

1 Which mammal's young is called a joey?

2 Which of these animals has the longer ears – a rabbit or a hare?

3 How tall is an ostrich – 1.3 metres, 2.1 metres or 2.7 metres?

4 What is the world's largest mammal and how much does it weigh?

5 What do fish breathe through?

1 Kangaroo 2 Hare 3 2.7 metres 4 Blue whale, weighing 150 tonnes 5 Gills

Why was Cinderella bad at basketball?

She had a pumpkin for a coach!

school notes

fun time

Monday

Tuesday

Wednesday

Thursday

Friday

it's the weekend

Saturday

Sunday

Girl power

Killer whales live in groups called pods. A pod is like a big family with parents, children and grandchildren. Usually the older females are in charge and decide which area is best to live in at each time of year.

Birthdays in March

8 Freddie Prinze Jr 1976
14 Einstein 1879
22 Keira Knightley 1985
22 Reese Witherspoon 1976
25 Sarah Jessica Parker 1965
27 Quentin Tarantino 1963
30 Norah Jones 1979
31 Ewan McGregor 1971

QUIZ

1 In the novel **Peter Pan**, where do the Lost Boys live?

2 Which animal knocked on the doors of the three little pigs?

3 What did the Grinch steal in December?

4 Which of the Seven Dwarfs is very shy?

5 What does the ugly duckling turn into?

answers
1 Neverland 2 The big bad wolf 3 Christmas 4 Bashful 5 Swan

How did the farmer mend his trousers?

With a cabbage patch

school notes

fun time

♥ Monday _____
_____
_____

♥ Tuesday _____
_____
_____

♥ Wednesday _____
_____
_____

♥ Thursday _____
_____
_____

♥ Friday _____
_____

it's the weekend

♥ Saturday

♥ Sunday

Tulip delight

The tulip is a well-known symbol of the Netherlands. Many tourists visit the country just to see the amazing fields of brightly coloured flowers and to buy souvenir bulbs from the many flower stalls.

More sheep than people!

Falkland Islands
New Zealand
Australia
Uruguay
Mongolia
Syria
Namibia
Iceland

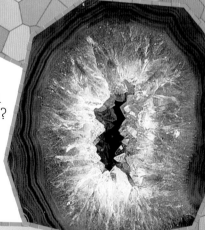

QUIZ

1 Which Christmas song was released by the 12 finalists of the 2003 TV contest **Pop Idol**?

2 Which boy band teamed up with Elton John on the hit "Sorry Seems To Be The Hardest Word"?

3 Which boy band was Justin Timberlake in before launching his solo career?

4 Which US pop goddess starred in the film **Crossroads**?

5 How many members does the boy band Westlife have?

answers
1 "Happy Christmas War Is Over", 2 Blue
3 N Sync, 4 Britney Spears, 5 Four

Why do elephants have trunks?
Because they don't have any pockets

school notes

fun time

Monday _____
_____
_____

Tuesday _____
_____
_____

Wednesday _____
_____
_____

Thursday _____
_____
_____

Friday _____
_____

it's the weekend

Saturday
_____
_____
_____

Sunday
_____
_____

Big baby!

A newborn harp seal weighs 12 kilograms – four times more than a human baby. It grows very quickly, doubling its weight in only five days.

celebrity nicknames

Elton John calls Rod Stewart 'Phyllis'...
...so Rod calls Elton 'Sharon'.

Guy Ritchie calls Madonna 'The Missus'.

Courtney Cox's childhood nickname was Cece.

Sting is so-called because he used to wear a wasp-striped T-shirt all the time.

Cameron Diaz was teased with the name 'Skeletor' because she was so skinny at school...

Nicole Kidman got stuck with the name 'Storky' because she was so tall.

Britney Spears is known as 'Pinkey'.

QUIZ

1 What gas makes up most of the atmosphere?

2 What planet shares its name with Mickey Mouse's pet dog?

3 What is the chemical symbol for water?

4 What nationality was the first man in space?

5 What does most of the brain consist of?

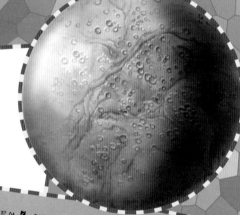

answers
1 Nitrogen 2 Pluto 3 H_2O 4 Russian 5 Water

How does a lion greet the other animals?

Pleased to eat you!

month

school notes

fun time

Monday _____
_____
_____
_____

Tuesday _____
_____
_____
_____

Wednesday _____
_____
_____
_____

Thursday _____
_____
_____
_____

Friday _____
_____
_____

it's the weekend

Saturday
_____
_____
_____
_____

Sunday
_____
_____
_____

Stone me!

Between 3000 and 1500BC, a circle of stones was created at Stonehenge in southern England. It is believed the huge pillars of stone were arranged so that they lined up with the rising and setting Sun. People could then study the Sun, Moon and changing seasons.

Birthdays in November

2 Nelly 1978
6 Ethan Hawke 1970
8 Jack Osbourne 1985
11 Leonardo DiCaprio 1974
11 Calista Flockhart 1964
11 Demi Moore 1962
13 Chris Noth 1954
14 Prince Charles 1948
22 Scarlett Johansson 1984
30 Ben Stiller 1965

QUIZ

1 Who is Miss Piggy madly in love with on **The Muppet Show**?

2 Who does Robbie Coltrane play in the Harry Potter films?

3 In which film did John Travolta sing of his love for Sandy?

4 What is the name of the dog in **The Magic Roundabout**?

5 In **The Jungle Book**, who is the bear who befriends Mowgli?

ANSWERS
1 Kermit the Frog 2 Hagrid 3 Grease
4 Dougal 5 Baloo

What is the definition of a caterpillar?

A worm in a fur coat!

school notes

fun time

♥ Monday _____

_____

_____

♥ Tuesday _____

_____

_____

♥ Wednesday _____

_____

_____

♥ Thursday _____

_____

_____

♥ Friday _____

_____

_____

it's the weekend

♥ Saturday

_____

_____

_____

♥ Sunday

_____

_____

Puppy love

In **Peter Pan**, the Darling children are looked after by a dog called Nana. When Mr Darling decides that Nana can't sleep in the children's nursery, the children fly away to Neverland. Mr Darling is so sorry that he sleeps outside in Nana's kennel until the children's safe return.

Speed sports

Sky diver – 1000 km/h
Racing motorbike – 300 km/h
Golf ball – 270 km/h
Tennis ball – 220 km/h
Skier – 210 km/h
Cricket ball – 160 km/h
Toboggan – 140 km/h
Greyhound – 67 km/h
Speed skater – 60 km/h
Sprinter – 37 km/h

QUIZ

1 What is the only animal mentioned in "Humpty Dumpty"?

2 What is the last animal in the rhyme "Hey Diddle Diddle"?

3 Which nursery rhyme character has an empty cupboard and a hungry dog?

4 Which type of fruit is in Little Jack Horner's pie?

5 Where was Dr Foster going?

answers
1 Horse 2 Dog 3 Old Mother Hubbard
4 Plum 5 Gloucester

Where do cows go on a Friday night?

To the mooovies!

school notes

fun time

Monday ———————————
———————————————————
———————————————————
———————————————————

Tuesday ———————————
———————————————————
———————————————————

Wednesday ——————————
———————————————————
———————————————————

Thursday ———————————
———————————————————
———————————————————

Friday —————————————
———————————————————
———————————————————

it's the weekend

Saturday

Sunday

Amazing art

Mona Lisa by Leonardo da Vinci (1452–1519) is the world's most famous painting. In 1911, it was stolen from the Louvre Museum, Paris. Six fakes were sold before it was recovered two years later.

Jobs you never knew existed

Alligator wrestler
Vermiculturist (worm farmer)
Apron cleaner (cleaning them for chefs)
Laughter therapist
Wrinkle chaser (making shoes smooth!)
Citrus fruit colourer
Odour judger (developing deodorant!)
Onion grader

QUIZ

1 For which film did Bryan Adams record the song "Everything I Do, I Do It For You"?

2 Which girl band was formed as a result of the 2002 TV contest Popstars: The Rivals?

3 What is the name of the pop star son of Julio Iglesias?

4 "I'll Be There For You" is the theme tune for which TV comedy show?

5 Which female trio had a hit with the song "The Tide Is High"?

answers
1 Robin Hood Prince Of Thieves
2 Girls Aloud 3 Enrique Iglesias
4 Friends 5 Atomic Kitten

Why did the spider buy a car?

So he could take it out for a spin!

school notes   fun time

Monday ——————————   ——————————
————————————————————   ——————————
————————————————————   ——————————

Tuesday ——————————   ——————————
————————————————————   ——————————
————————————————————   ——————————

Wednesday ——————————   ——————————
————————————————————   ——————————
————————————————————   ——————————

Thursday ——————————   ——————————
————————————————————   ——————————
————————————————————   ——————————

Friday ——————————   ——————————
————————————————————   ——————————

it's the weekend

Saturday ——————————
————————————————————
————————————————————
————————————————————

Sunday ——————————
————————————————————
————————————————————
————————————————————

Butter-flies

The origin of the word 'butterfly' is unclear. It may have first been used to describe the 'butter' colour of male brimstone butterflies. When 'butterfly' was used to describe the group of insects, brimstones took a new name – probably after the yellow mineral, sulphur.

Fastest animals

Peregrine falcon – 270 km/h
Canvasback duck – 110 km/h
Sailfish – 109 km/h
Cheetah – 100 km/h
Pronghorn antelope – 100 km/h
Swift – 95 km/h
Gazelle – 80 km/h
Lion – 80 km/h
Race horse – 70 km/h
Jackrabbit – 70 km/h

QUIZ

1 Which fictional bear lives in the town of Nutwood?

2 Who fell in love with Romeo in the city of Verona?

3 Which Charles Dickens novel features a villain called Bill Sikes?

4 Who is Harry Potter's schoolboy enemy in J K Rowling's famous novels?

5 Where in England do the Wombles live?

answers
1 Rupert 2 Juliet 3 Oliver Twist
4 Draco Malfoy 5 Wimbledon Common

What does an angry spider do?

It goes up the wall

school notes

fun time

Monday _____

_____

_____

_____

Tuesday _____

_____

_____

Wednesday _____

_____

Thursday _____

_____

_____

Friday _____

_____

it's the weekend

Saturday _____

_____

_____

_____

Sunday _____

_____

_____

Spider speed

The house spider can run at nearly 2 kilometres an hour. That's like a human sprinter running 800 metres in 10 seconds, which is much faster than any Olympic athlete.

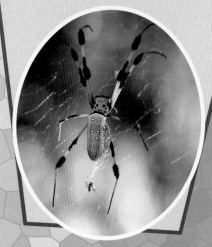

Birthdays in October

3 Gwen Stefani 1969
5 Nikki Hilton 1983
5 Kate Winslet 1975
7 Simon Cowell 1959
8 Matt Damon 1970
9 Sharon Osbourne 1952
14 Usher 1979
17 Eminem 1972
17 Wyclef Jean 1972
27 Kelly Osbourne 1984

QUIZ

1. What do marsupials carry their young in?
2. Which flower shares its name with the last shade of the rainbow?
3. What name is shared by a young beaver and a young cat?
4. Is the skin of a polar bear black, white or pink?
5. What is a female sheep called?

1 Pouch 2 Violet 3 Kitten 4 Black, only the fur is white 5 Ewe

How to elephants talk to each other?

By 'elephone!

month

school notes

fun time

♥ Monday _____

♥ Tuesday _____

♥ Wednesday _____

♥ Thursday _____

♥ Friday _____

it's the weekend

Saturday

Sunday

Lady liberty

The Statue of Liberty in the USA measures 46 metres in height. It was a gift from the people of France and was opened in 1886 as a monument to American Independence.

Funny body facts

You shed about 18 kilograms of dead skin in your lifetime.

After the age of 18, we lose over 1000 brain cells EACH DAY!

All the nerves in your body laid end to end would stretch about 75 kilometres.

Earwax has an unpleasant smell to stop insects entering your ear!

You lose about 80 hairs from your head every day.

Tooth enamel is the hardest substance made by animals.

QUIZ

1 What type of marine creature is the TV and film hero, Flipper?

2 Which DC. refers to the name given to a vicar's neckwear?

3 What are the first and second letters of the Greek alphabet?

4 What is the Beano character Desperate Dan's hometown called?

5 Zwanzig is German for which number?

answers
1 Dolphin 2 Dog collar 3 Alpha and Beta 4 Cactusville 5 20

What's a vampire's favourite sport?

Batminton!

school notes

fun time

Monday _____

_____

_____

_____

Tuesday _____

_____

_____

_____

Wednesday _____

_____

_____

_____

Thursday _____

_____

_____

_____

Friday _____

_____

_____

it's the weekend

Saturday

Sunday

Brainy birdy

The parrot is one of the brainiest birds. It can be trained to copy human speech. Some can even count and name objects!

Birthdays in May

2 David Beckham 1975
6 Tony Blair 1953
8 Enrique Iglesias 1975
10 Bono 1960
11 Holly Valance 1983
16 David Boreanaz 1971
25 Mike Myers 1963
27 Andre 3000 1975
28 Kylie Minogue 1968
29 Noel Gallagher 1967

QUIZ

1 What is the name of the little boy in the Christmas story, **The Snowman**?

2 Which house does Harry Potter belong to at Hogwart's School?

3 Which A word means a book written by a person about their own life?

4 In which country is the novel **The Hunchback of Notre Dame** set?

5 Who lost her sheep in a nursery rhyme?

Answers
1 James 2 Gryffindor 3 Autobiography 4 France 5 Little Bo Peep

What do you call a deer with no eyes?

No eye deer!

month

school notes

fun time

Monday

Tuesday

Wednesday

Thursday

Friday

it's the weekend

Saturday

Sunday

Choctastic!

Chocolate originally comes from South America and is one of the most popular foods ever. The Swiss eat the most chocolate with the average person consuming 10 kilograms each year!

Countries that have had women leaders

Sri Lanka
India
Israel
Argentina
Philippines
UK
Portugal
Iceland
Norway

QUIZ

1. Alphabetically, which is the last star sign?
2. Alpha, Bravo, Charlie, Delta. What comes next?
3. In which US city does Batman fight crime?
4. Which chess piece can only move diagonally?
5. How many cents are in a dollar?

answers
1 Virgo 2 Echo 3 Gotham City 4 The bishop 5 100

Why won't the Earth come to an end?

Because it's round!

school notes

fun time

Monday _____
_____
_____

Tuesday _____
_____
_____

Wednesday _____
_____
_____

Thursday _____
_____
_____

Friday _____
_____

it's the weekend

Saturday _____
_____
_____
_____
_____

Sunday _____
_____
_____
_____

Eye eye!

Kittens should stay with their mother until they are eight weeks old. Their eyes are closed for the first week of their lives. Although born with grey-blue eyes, they change to their adult colour at 12 weeks old.

celeb siblings

Paris **and** Nicky **Hilton**

Natasha **and** Daniel **Bedingfield**

Dido **and** Rollo (Faithless) **Armstrong**

Dannii **and** Kylie **Minogue**

Noel **and** Liam **Gallagher**

Joely **and** Natasha **Richardson**

Jonathon **and** Paul **Ross**

Jack **and** Kelly **Osbourne**

Serena **and** Venus **Williams**

Lady Victoria **and** Isabella **Hervey**

QUIZ

1. Which star of the film **Mission Impossible** was married to Nicole Kidman?
2. Who was the second man to walk on the moon?
3. Which tennis star married Andre Agassi in 2001?
4. What is the first name of the character played by David Duchovny in **The X Files**?
5. In which year was Queen Elizabeth II born?

1 Tom Cruise 2 Buzz Aldrin 3 Steffi Graf 4 Fox 5 1926

What can't be answered with a yes?

Are you asleep?

school notes

fun time

♥ Monday _____

_____

_____

♥ Tuesday _____

_____

♥ Wednesday _____

_____

♥ Thursday _____

_____

♥ Friday _____

_____

it's the weekend

♥ Saturday _____

_____

_____

_____

♥ Sunday _____

Strike seven

Roy Sullivan is the only man to be struck by lightning seven times, but there is no explanation! Between 1942 and 1977, he had his hair set alight and suffered severe injuries to his body. Amazingly he survived every single hit!

BizaRRe UK laws

York – it is legal to shoot a Scotsman if you use a bow and arrow. Except on Sunday.

Countrywide – it is illegal to be drunk in possession of a cow.

London – you can't move cows down the high street between 10 a.m. and 7 p.m.

London Zoo – you are forbidden from giving any of the animals a cigarette.

QUIZ

1 Which type of animal was forever trying to catch Roadrunner?

2 Who starred in the hit film I, Robot and Men in Black?

3 Who was the first actor to play James Bond in a film?

4 Who asks the questions on the TV game show The Weakest Link?

5 What is the Flintstones' family pet called?

answers
1 Coyote 2 Will Smith 3 Sean Connery 4 Anne Robinson 5 Dino

Why was the butcher worried?

His job was at steak!

month

school notes

fun time

♥ Monday _____
_____
_____
_____

♥ Tuesday _____
_____
_____

♥ Wednesday _____
_____
_____

♥ Thursday _____
_____
_____

♥ Friday _____
_____
_____

it's the weekend

♥ Saturday
_____
_____
_____
_____

♥ Sunday
_____
_____
_____

Best mates

Puppies and kittens can be great friends if they are brought up together from when they are very young – they will feel like they are brothers and sisters!

celeb holiday spots

Gwen Stefani – Las Vegas
Tamzin Outhwaite – Barcelona
George Clooney – South of France
Estelle – Miami
Sienna Miller – Marrakech (Morocco)
Hugh Grant – Sardinia
Kate Moss – St Tropez
Gwyneth Paltrow – Mexico
Ronaldo – Formentera
Beyonce – St Barts, Caribbean

QUIZ

1 With which group did Annie Lennox first enjoy chart success?

2 What is Elvis Presley's mansion in Memphis called?

3 In 2005, with which song did Westlife win **Record of the Year**?

4 What was the first James Bond theme tune performed by Shirley Bassey?

5 Where do Stereophonics come from?

Answers
1 The Tourists 2 Graceland
3 "You Lift Me Up" 4 "Goldfinger" 5 Wales

What do you call a crate of ducks?

A box of quackers!

school notes

fun time

Monday _____

_____

_____

Tuesday _____

_____

_____

Wednesday _____

_____

_____

Thursday _____

_____

_____

Friday _____

_____

it's the weekend

Saturday _____

Sunday _____

Forest fun

Kenneth Grahame was born in 1859. He originally wrote **The Wind in the Willows** for his son, but it is now a classic, loved by children and adults around the world.

RAT

Songs about the rain

It's Raining Men – Geri Halliwell

Raindrops Keep Falling on My Head – B J Thomas

The Rain (Supa Dupa Fly) – Missy Elliott

Rainy Daze – Mary J Blige

Singing in the Rain – Gene Kelly

Rain – Madonna

Rainy Days and Mondays – The Carpenters

Here Comes the Rain Again – The Eurythmics

I Can't Stand the Rain – Tina Turner

I'm Only Happy When it Rains – Garbage

QUIZ

1 Which Dickens' novel features the character of Little Nell?

2 Which soccer player released a book entitled **My Side** in 2,003?

3 Which adventure novel introduced readers to Captain Nemo?

4 In a nursery rhyme, who "sat amongst the cinders"?

5 In the Harry Potter stories, what species of owl is Hedwig?

answers
1 The Old Curiosity Shop 2 David Beckham
3 20,000 Leagues Under the Sea
4 Little Polly Flinders 5 Snowy owl

Why did the foal cough?

Because he was a little horse!

school notes

fun time

♥ Monday _____

_____

_____

_____

♥ Tuesday _____

_____

_____

_____

♥ Wednesday _____

_____

_____

_____

♥ Thursday _____

_____

_____

_____

♥ Friday _____

_____

it's the weekend

♥ Saturday

_____

♥ Sunday

Tiger terror

Siberian tigers are great predators. The male is the biggest of the big cats, measuring 3.2 metres in length and weighing 300 kilograms. There are only about 400 left in the wild today.

Birthdays in February

7 Ashton Kutcher 1978
8 Seth Green 1974
11 Kelly Rowland 1981
11 Jennifer Aniston 1969
12 Judy Blume 1938
13 Robbie Williams 1974
15 Matt Groening 1954
17 Paris Hilton 1981
21 Charlotte Church 1986

QUIZ

1 In which month is Thanksgiving Day celebrated in the United States?

2 What is the traditional occupation of a leprechaun?

3 Who is the voice of Alex the lion in the 2005 animation, **Madagascar**?

4 Which five-letter word can go after egg and before shock?

5 What is a motorway called in German?

1 November 2 Cobbler or shoemaker 3 Ben Stiller 4 Shell 5 Autobahn

What is a spider's favourite food?

Corn on the cobweb!

school notes

fun time

Monday _____
_____
_____

Tuesday _____
_____

Wednesday _____
_____
_____

Thursday _____
_____
_____

Friday _____
_____
_____

it's the weekend

Saturday

Sunday

Snow deep

The place with the most snow isn't actually the North or South Pole, but the west coast of the United States. The deepest snowfall ever was in California in 1911. Snow lay 11.46 metres deep – enough to bury a house.

world's hottest cities

Djibouti, Djibouti
Timbuktu, Mali
Tirunelveli, India
Tuticorin, India
Aden, South Yemen
Madurai, India
Naimey, Niger
Tiruchirapalli, India
Khartoum, Sudan
Omdurman, Sudan

QUIZ

1 Which African country was invaded by Italy in 1935 and aided by Bob Geldof 50 years later?

2 Which S is the capital of the Andalusia region of Spain?

3 Which country is home to over half the world's tigers?

4 What are the two most famous universities in the UK?

5 In which country was denim first made?

answers
1 Ethiopia 2 Seville 3 India 4 Cambridge and Oxford 5 France

What's black, white and noisy?

A zebra with a drum kit

month

school notes

fun time

Monday _____
_____
_____
_____

Tuesday _____
_____
_____

Wednesday _____
_____
_____

Thursday _____
_____
_____

Friday _____
_____

it's the weekend

Saturday
_____
_____
_____

Sunday

Stripy style

No one knows why zebras have stripes. Each has a unique pattern and zebras can recognize another member of its herd simply by its pattern.

celeb businesses

Jay-Z – 40/40 sports bar, NY
Kylie Minogue – Love Kylie underwear
Paris Hilton – Club Paris, Orlando
Moby – Teany teahouse, NY
J-Lo – Madre's restaurant, California
Elle Macpherson – Intimates underwear
Liz Hurley – Swimwear
Victoria Beckham – Rock and Republic jeans
Johnny Depp – Viper Room club, Hollywood
Britney Spears – NYLA restaurant, NY

QUIZ

1. What does a seismograph record the intensity of?
2. Which is the largest tendon in the human body?
3. Which organ of the body produces the hormone, insulin?
4. As used by a teacher, what is the common name for calcium carbonate?
5. Which gas solidifies to form dry ice?

answers
1 Earthquakes 2 Achilles tendon 3 Pancreas 4 Chalk 5 Carbon dioxide

How do snails keep their shells shiny?

They use snail varnish

school notes

fun time

Monday ——————————————
————————————————————————
————————————————————————

Tuesday ——————————————
————————————————————————
————————————————————————

Wednesday ————————————
————————————————————————
————————————————————————

Thursday —————————————
————————————————————————
————————————————————————

Friday ———————————————
————————————————————————
————————————————————————

it's the weekend

Saturday

Sunday

Tutankha-tomb

The solid gold death mask of Tutankhamun was found in the Valley of Kings, Egypt. The entrance was guarded, but it was frequently robbed. One tomb that remained untouched was that of Tutankhamun.

Birthday in september

4 Beyoncé Knowles 1981

8 Pink 1979

9 Hugh Grant 1960

15 Prince Harry 1984

18 Lance Armstrong 1971

21 Liam Gallagher 1972

25 Catherine Zeta Jones 1969

25 Will Smith 1968

27 Avril Lavigne 1984

28 Gwyneth Paltrow 1972

QUIZ

1 Down the Rabbit Hole is the first chapter of which novel?

2 The film The Slipper and the Rose was based on which popular fairytale?

3 Who owned a dog called Jip and a pig called Gub?

4 What connects the author Helen Fielding and the film star Renee Zellweger?

5 Which famous artist painted the ceiling of the Sistine Chapel in the Vatican?

answers

1 Alice's Adventures in Wonderland
2 Cinderella 3 Dr Doolittle Scott
4 Bridget Jones's Diary
5 Michelangelo

Which breed is Dracula's dog?

A blood hound!

school notes

fun time

Monday _____

_____

_____

_____

Tuesday _____

_____

_____

_____

Wednesday _____

_____

_____

_____

Thursday _____

_____

_____

_____

Friday _____

_____

_____

_____

it's the weekend

Saturday _____

_____

_____

_____

Sunday _____

_____

_____

_____

Fiendish fish

Great whites are the scariest sharks ever! At about 6 to 7 metres long, they can speed through water at 30 kilometres an hour – speedily chasing their prey, which can sometimes be humans!

Fab bird facts

The Andean condor can live to be over 70 years old.

Ducks (and other birds) have an 'eggtooth' on their beak to chip out of their shell. It falls off after hatching.

Male greater roadrunners give females a present of a lizard to attract them as a mate.

Hummingbirds have rare talents – they can hover and fly backwards.

Pelican chicks can tell their parents if they're too hot or cold while they're still inside their egg.

QUIZ

1 Who won an Oscar® for Best actress in the film **Moonstruck**?

2 **Holby City** is a spin off from which medical drama?

3 Which police TV series is set at Sun Hill Station?

4 In the animated version of **Robin Hood**, which animal is Robin?

5 What kind of fish is Nemo in the animation, **Finding Nemo**?

1 Cher 2 Casualty 3 The Bill
4 Fox 5 Clownfish

Why are ghosts such poor magicians?

You can see right through their tricks!

month

school notes

fun time

Monday

Tuesday

Wednesday

Thursday

Friday

it's the weekend

Saturday

Sunday

Monsterous!

The director of Pixar's **Monsters, Inc**, Pete Docter, came up with the idea for the film as he believed there were monsters in his wardrobe as a child. The film was no easy task – Sully has 2,320,413 computer-animated hairs on his body.

Stars of the West End

David Schwimmer – Some Girls

Gwyneth Paltrow – Proof

Kim Cattrall – Whose Life Is It Anyway?

Val Kilmer – The Postman Always Rings Twice

Kevin Spacey – The Philadelphia Story

Ewan McGregor – Guys and Dolls

Nicole Kidman – The Blue Room

Madonna – Up For Grabs

Christian Slater – One Flew Over The Cuckoo's Nest

Matt Damon – This Is Our Youth

QUIZ

1 What was the first No. 1 hit for singer Tom Jones?

2 Which nationality was the composer Giamaco Puccini?

3 In a song from the musical **My Fair Lady**, in which country does rain fall?

4 Which country and western star opened a theme park called Dollywood?

5 On whose poems was the stage musical **Cats** based?

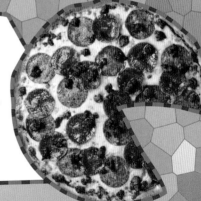

answers
1 "It's Not Unusual." 2 Italian 3 Spain 4 Dolly Parton 5 T S Eliot

How long do chickens work?

Around the cluck!

school notes

fun time

Monday

Tuesday

Wednesday

Thursday

Friday

it's the weekend

Saturday

Sunday

Gutsy girl!

Mary Read dressed in man's clothes, so she could become a sailor. When pirates captured her ship, she was taken prisoner. She joined the pirates and became one of the bravest female pirates of all time.

Celebrity exes

Britney Spears **and Justin Timberlake**
Russell Crowe and Sharon Stone
Juliette Lewis **and Leonardo DiCaprio**
Matthew McConaghy and Penelope Cruz
Geri Halliwell **and Fred Durst**
Ben Affleck and Gwyneth Paltrow
Minnie Driver **and Matt Damon**
Matthew Perry and Julia Roberts
Nicole Kidman **and Tom Cruise**
Matt Dillon and Cameron Diaz

QUIZ

1 Which London building is home to the Whispering Gallery?

2 Which is the largest castle in Wales, and also the name of a cheese?

3 Which is the only country to be on the border of Denmark?

4 Which group of islands does Ibiza belong to?

5 In which US state is Las Vegas?

answers
1 St Paul's Cathedral 2 Caerphilly 3 Germany 4 The Balearics 5 Nevada

What do wild animals sing at Christmas?

Jungle bells

school notes

fun time

Monday _____

_____

_____

_____

Tuesday _____

_____

_____

_____

Wednesday _____

_____

_____

_____

Thursday _____

_____

_____

_____

Friday _____

_____

_____

it's the weekend

Saturday _____

Sunday _____

Clever cover

The fawn has huge ears, big eyes and a strong sense of smell to detect danger. Its coat is dappled with white spots on brown fur. It blends in with patches of sunlight on the ground, making the fawn difficult to see.

Birthday in January

3 Michael Schumacher 1969

5 Marilyn Manson 1969

11 Mary J Blige 1971

13 Orlando Bloom 1977

16 Kate Moss 1974

17 Jim Carrey 1962

24 Mischa Barton 1986

28 Elijah Wood 1981

29 Heather Graham 1970

31 Justin Timberlake 1981

QUIZ

1 Anne Shirley is the main character in which L M Montgomery novel?

2 On whose fairytale was the Disney movie **The Little Mermaid** based?

3 What type of animal is Jeremy Fisher in the Beatrix Potter stories?

4 In which year was Christopher Paolini, the author of **Eragon**, born?

5 Which doctor created the character, the Grinch?

answers
1 Anne of Green Gables
2 Hans Christian Andersen 3 Frog
4 1983 5 Dr Seuss

What's good to eat in the bath?

Sponge cake

school notes

fun time

Monday ─────────────────
──────────────────────────
──────────────────────────
──────────────────────────

Tuesday ─────────────────
──────────────────────────
──────────────────────────

Wednesday ───────────────
──────────────────────────
──────────────────────────

Thursday ────────────────
──────────────────────────
──────────────────────────

Friday ──────────────────
──────────────────────────

it's the weekend

Saturday
──────────────────────
──────────────────────
──────────────────────

Sunday
──────────────────────
──────────────────────
──────────────────────

Lava Loa

The world's biggest volcano is Mauna Loa in Hawaii. It rises 9000 metres from the sea floor. A huge 80 percent of this monstrous volcano is actually below sea level.

Animal comparisons

The giant squid has the biggest eye – larger than a human head!

The blue whale is the world's biggest creature – with a heart the size of a small car.

The puma can jump higher than any other animal – well over 4 metres in the air.

The giraffe is the world's tallest animal. Males measure up to 6 metres in height.

The golden poison frog is the most poisonous creature – with enough poison to kill 10 to 20 humans.

QUIZ

1 How many planets are there in our Solar System?

2 What is the common name for the olfactory organ?

3 How is two-fifths expressed as a percentage?

4 How many equal angles are there in an isosceles triangle?

5 How many sides does a heptagon have?

1 Nine 2 Nose 3 40 percent 4 Two 5 Seven

Why did the burglar take a shower?

Because he wanted to make a clean getaway!

school notes

fun time

♥ Monday _____
_____
_____

♥ Tuesday _____
_____
_____

♥ Wednesday _____
_____
_____

♥ Thursday _____
_____
_____

♥ Friday _____
_____
_____

it's the weekend

Saturday

Sunday

Mystic mog

People are very superstitious about black cats. They often appear in tales about witches and wizards. Some people once believed that cats could cast their own spells!

world's driest cities

Antofagasta, Chile

Luxor, Egypt

Aswan, Egypt

Asyut, Egypt

Callao, Peru

Trujillo, Peru

Suez, Egypt

Giza, Egypt

Cairo, Egypt

Zagazig, Egypt

QUIZ

1 The TV shows **Ally McBeal** and **Cheers** are both set in which city?

2 Which monster was captured on Skull Island and transported to New York City?

3 In the film **A Fish Called Wanda**, which actress played Wanda?

4 Which animated crime-fighting group do Blossom, Bubbles and Buttercup belong to?

5 Which foe of Batman is often shown carrying an umbrella?

answers
1 Boston 2 King Kong 3 Jamie Lee Curtis
4 The Powerpuff Girls 5 The Penguin

Why can't a bike stand up by itself?

Because it's two tyred!

school notes

fun time

Monday _____

_____

_____

Tuesday _____

_____

_____

Wednesday _____

_____

_____

Thursday _____

_____

_____

Friday _____

_____

_____

it's the weekend

Saturday

Sunday

Bubbly bear

First published in 1926, A A Milne's **Winnie the Pooh** is an all-time classic. Winnie the Pooh's official birthday is 21 August 1921 – the day Christopher Robin is given Pooh for his first birthday.

Amazing foliage

The Kigelia africana tree is called the sausage tree because of the shape of its fruit.

To spread its seeds, the fruit of the sandbox tree (South America) explodes with a loud bang and scatters seeds up to 4.5 metres!

One plant in Bolivia takes up to 150 years to bloom, and then dies straight afterwards.

The starfish flower of Africa looks like a starfish in the sand, but smells of dead flesh.

A kind of mimosa plant plays dead if you touch it. After about 10 minutes it revives itself.

QUIZ

1 Which is the largest wild carnivore native to the British Isles?

2 How many legs does the average lobster have?

3 What is the name given to a female foal?

4 What is the largest amphibian in the world?

5 What shape is a bee's honeycomb?

answers
1 Badger 2 Ten 3 Filly
4 Giant salamander 5 Hexagonal

What did the balloon say to the pin?

"Hi, Buster!"

school notes

fun time

Monday

Tuesday

Wednesday

Thursday

Friday

it's the weekend

Saturday

Sunday

Dark day

When the Moon hides the Sun, there is an eclipse. Every few years, the Earth, Sun and Moon line up in space so that the Moon comes directly between the Earth and the Sun. Sunlight cannot reach Earth, so it seems like night.

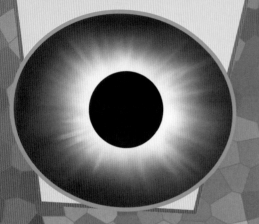

weird superstitions

Nigeria – it's unlucky to sweep your house at night.

Poland – lilac in the house is a sign of impending death.

Ireland – it's lucky to spill drink on the ground.

Scotland – it's unlucky to carry a spade through the house.

Holland – red-headed people bring bad luck.

Ibiza – don't allow a priest on a fishing boat!

Japan – don't pick up a comb with the teeth facing your body.

QUIZ

Can you identify these four food types?

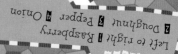

answers
Left to right 1 Raspberry
2 Doughnut 3 Pepper 4 Onion

Why did the child study in the plane?

He wanted a higher education!

school notes

Monday _____
_____
_____

Tuesday _____
_____
_____

Wednesday _____
_____
_____

Thursday _____
_____
_____

Friday _____
_____

it's the weekend

Saturday _____
_____
_____
_____

Sunday _____
_____
_____
_____

Fit feline

The puma is a great athlete and can spring 2 metres into a tree with ease. However, it is not classed as one of the seven species of big cats. The puma cannot roar – instead, it makes an ear-piercing scream.

Birthdays in June

4 Angelina Jolie 1975
7 Anna Kournikova 1981
9 Natalie Portman 1981
9 Johnny Depp 1963
10 Liz Hurley 1965
13 Mary-Kate and Ashley Olsen 1986
15 Courtney Cox 1964
20 Nicole Kidman 1967
21 Prince William 1982
27 Tobey Maguire 1975

QUIZ

1 In which European country is the town of Spa famous for its mineral springs?

2 Which US state does the Arctic Circle pass through?

3 What is the name of the river that runs through the Grand Canyon?

4 What is the world's largest country with an X in its name?

5 Which is the largest Greek island?

Answers
1 Belgium 2 Alaska 3 Colorado 4 Mexico 5 Crete

Why was the broom late?

It over swept!

school notes

fun time

Monday _____

_____

_____

Tuesday _____

_____

_____

Wednesday _____

_____

_____

Thursday _____

_____

_____

Friday _____

_____

_____

it's the weekend

Saturday

Sunday

Arty aussies

Sydney Opera House had to be built twice. The unique shape of the roof was so advanced for its time that builders had to start work before the building materials had even been invented! When they realized that the roof would be too heavy, they had to blow up the foundations and start again.

World's wettest cities

Monrovia, Liberia
Moulmein, Burma (Myanmar)
Padang, Sumatra, Indonesia
Conkary, Guinea
Bogor, Java, Indonesia
Douala, Cameroon
Cayenne, French Guiana
Freetown, Sierra Leone
Ambon, Indonesia
Mangalore, India

QUIZ

1 Which tailless breed of cat comes from the Isle of Man?

2 Where are the withers on a horse's body?

3 By which year did the dodo become extinct?

4 What is the nationl bird of the US?

5 Which animal would you find in a holt?

answers
1 Manx 2 Between the shoulders 3 1680
4 Bald eagle 5 Otter

What runs but never walks?

Water!

school notes

fun time

Monday ——————————————
——————————————————————
——————————————————————
——————————————————————

Tuesday ——————————————
——————————————————————
——————————————————————
——————————————————————

Wednesday ————————————
——————————————————————
——————————————————————
——————————————————————

Thursday —————————————
——————————————————————
——————————————————————
——————————————————————

Friday ———————————————
——————————————————————
——————————————————————

it's the weekend

Saturday

Sunday

Petite panda

A newborn giant panda is smaller than your hand, white all over, has almost no fur and its eyes are tightly closed. However, just six months later it is big enough to be munching on its favourite food – bamboo!

Unusual festivals

Spain – La Tomatina – people throw tomatoes at each other.

USA – Doodah Parade – a festival of bad taste and tackiness.

Norway – Grandmothers' Festival – bungee-jumping and skydiving for grannies.

India – Gotmaar Festival – people throw rocks at each other.

Mexico – Day of the Dead – people eat chocolate coffins at gravesides.

USA – Running of the Sheep – prizes are given for the ugliest sheep and prettiest ewe.

QUIZ

1 Which of the Seven Dwarfs has a three-letter name?

2 Which character in the film **Troy** was played by Orlando Bloom?

3 In which novel trilogy would you find Lyra Belacqua and Will Parry?

4 Which type of bird taught Dr Doolittle to talk to the animals?

5 Who created the Mr Men?

answers
1 Doc 2 Paris 3 His Dark Materials 4 Parrot 5 Roger Hargreaves

How do you make milk shake?

Give it a good scare!

school notes

fun time

Monday _____

_____

_____

Tuesday _____

_____

_____

Wednesday _____

_____

_____

Thursday _____

_____

_____

Friday _____

_____

_____

_____

_____

_____

_____

_____

_____

_____

_____

_____

_____

_____

_____

_____

_____

it's the weekend

Saturday _____

_____

_____

_____

Sunday _____

_____

_____

_____

Royal party

Queen Elizabeth II has travelled further than any other British monarch, visiting many Commonwealth people. She celebrated her Golden Jubilee, 50 years as Queen, in 2002 with spectacular parties and concerts.

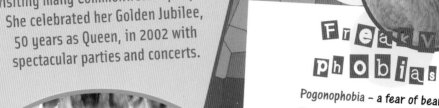

Freaky phobias

Pogonophobia – a fear of beards
Tonsurphobia – a fear of haircuts
Anthophobia – a fear of roses
Siderodromophobia – a fear of train travel
Mysophobia – a fear of germs
Brontophobia – a fear of thunder
Hydrophobia – a fear of water
Genuphobia – a fear of knees
Clinophobia – a fear of going to bed
Alektorophobia – a fear of chickens

QUIZ

Can you identify these stars of music and cinema?

Left to right: 1 Tom Cruise 2 Marilyn Monroe 3 Will Smith 4 Elvis Presley

answers

What's red, flies and wobbles?

A jelly-copter!

month

school notes

fun time

♥ Monday _____

♥ Tuesday _____

♥ Wednesday _____

♥ Thursday _____

♥ Friday _____

it's the weekend

♥ Saturday

♥ Sunday

Mini Rex

The great predator, Tyrannosaurus rex, was up to 13 metres in length, 6 metres in height and 6 tonnes in weight! Its jaws were wide enough to swallow the equivalent of an average 10-year-old child whole!

Birthdays in April

7 Jackie Chan 1954
9 Rachel Stevens 1978
11 Joss Stone 1987
14 Sarah Michelle Gellar 1977
17 Victoria Beckham 1974
18 Melissa Joan Hart 1976
19 Maria Sharapova 1987
19 Hayden Christensen 1981
25 Renee Zellweger 1969
30 Kirsten Dunst 1982

QUIZ

1 What is the name of the yeasted bread eaten with Indian food?

2 Which animal represents a zoo on a British ordinance survey map?

3 In the cartoon, what is the name of the Flintstones' daughter?

4 Which country will host the 2012 Olympic Games?

5 Who wrote the novel Robinson Crusoe?

1 Naan bread 2 Elephant 3 Pebbles 4 Great Britain 5 Daniel Defoe

"Waiter, this soup tastes funny"

"Then why aren't you laughing!"

month

school notes

fun time

♥ Monday

♥ Tuesday

♥ Wednesday

♥ Thursday

♥ Friday

it's the weekend

Saturday

Sunday

Great genius

Albert Einstein was the greatest scientist of the 20th century. After he died in 1955, his brain was donated to science to see if it gave any clues as to why he was so intelligent. It turned out to be wider than average, so perhaps it had a greater thinking capacity!

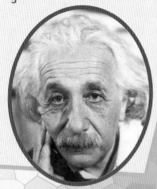

weird cures not to try!

Put a cork under your pillow at night to cure cramp.

Carry a dead shrew in your pocket to keep away rheumatism.

Throw a dung beetle over your shoulder to get rid of stomach ache.

Rub warts with the chopped-off head of an eel to make them go.

Tie a bag containing a hairy caterpillar round your neck to cure whooping cough.

Wear a tooth taken from a live mole to get rid of toothache.

QUIZ

1 Which boy's name is also the name for a rabbit's home?

2 Which sleepy mammal is also the name of one of the seven deadly sins?

3 Is an anchovy a flower, a fish, a frog or a fruit?

4 Which species of fly is sometimes called a daddy-longlegs?

5 What does the mammal, a pinniped, have instead of feet?

answers
1 Warren 2 Sloth 3 Fish
4 Crane fly 5 Flippers

What do snowmen eat for breakfast?

Frosties!

school notes

fun time

♥ Monday _____
_____
_____
_____

♥ Tuesday _____
_____
_____
_____

♥ Wednesday _____
_____
_____
_____

♥ Thursday _____
_____
_____
_____

♥ Friday _____
_____
_____

it's the weekend

♥ Saturday

♥ Sunday

Clever clogs

Dolphins are intelligent mammals. They can learn many tricks and stunts, like leaping through hoops, knocking balls with their beaks, and giving people rides on their backs. They can recognize many different shapes, count and mimic sounds.

Bizarre US laws

Alaska – it's illegal to look at a moose through the window of an aeroplane.

Ohio – pets must have lights on their tails at night.

Kentucky – it's illegal to carry an ice-cream cone in your pocket.

Minnesota – dog owners will be fined if their pet chases a cat up a telegraph pole.

Illinois – bees are forbidden from flying over the town.

Oklahoma – it is illegal to get a fish drunk.

Nebraska – barbers may not eat onions between 7 a.m. and 7 p.m.

QUIZ

1 What is the name of Scotland's largest loch?

2 Is the cross on the Norwegian flag red, white or blue?

3 In which US city can the Golden Gate bridge be found?

4 How many oceans are there in the world – two, four or six?

5 Tenerife and Lanzarote belong to which island group?

answers
1 Loch Lomond 2 Blue 3 San Francisco 4 Four 5 The Canaries

What's brown and sticky?

A stick

month

school notes

fun time

Monday _____

Tuesday _____

Wednesday _____

Thursday _____

Friday _____

it's the weekend

Saturday _____

Sunday

Pretty petal

Bluebells were recently voted the UK's most popular wild flowers. The second part of the bluebell's Latin name, **non-scriptus**, means unlettered because the petals are not marked in any way.

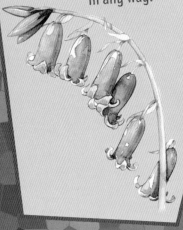

sound fishy!

A starfish will grow a new leg if it loses one.

The largest jellyfish can grow tentacles up to 37 metres long.

The smallest fish is the goby, which can be smaller than a housefly.

The ocean sunfish is about 60 million times bigger than its babies.

The archerfish shoots its prey upwards with a squirt of water.

The African lungfish can live for up to three years buried in mud.

QUIZ

1. By which name is a domesticated polecat also known?

2. What was the first bird mentioned by name in the Bible?

3. Which breed of dog's name means badger hound?

4. Which bird lays the largest egg in proportion to the size of its body?

5. How many legs does a starfish have?

answers

1 Ferret 2 Raven 3 Dachshund
4 Kiwi 5 Five

Why did the carpenter go to his GP?

He had a saw hand!

school notes

fun time

Monday ―――――――――――――
――――――――――――――――――――
――――――――――――――――――――

Tuesday ――――――――――――
――――――――――――――――――――
――――――――――――――――――――

Wednesday ――――――――――
――――――――――――――――――――
――――――――――――――――――――

Thursday ――――――――――――
――――――――――――――――――――
――――――――――――――――――――

Friday ―――――――――――――――
――――――――――――――――――――
――――――――――――――――――――

it's the weekend

Saturday ―――――――――――――
――――――――――――――――――――
――――――――――――――――――――
――――――――――――――――――――
――――――――――――――――――――
――――――――――――――――――――

Sunday ――――――――――――――
――――――――――――――――――――
――――――――――――――――――――
――――――――――――――――――――
――――――――――――――――――――

Nifty nap

Swifts spend their lives on the wing – they even sleep in the air, roosting at 1000 to 2000 metres above the ground.

Pop songs about summer

Seasons in the Sun – **Westlife**
Summer of '69 – **Bryan Adams**
Summer Girls – **Lyte Funkie Ones**
Here Comes the Sun – **The Beatles**
Summer Nights – **Grease**
Summer of Love – **Steps**
Sunshine – **Gabrielle**
Summer Bunnies – **R Kelly**
Summer Son – **Texas**
Summer Night City – **Abba**

QUIZ

1 Which novel features an escaped convict called Magwitch?

2 What type of bird is Fawkes in the Harry Potter stories?

3 Which author was portrayed by Nicole Kidman in **The Hours**?

4 Which Irish poet wrote **Digging** and **Follower**?

5 Which novel features the character of Mrs Doasyouwouldbedoneby?

1 Great Expectations 2 Phoenix
3 Virginia Woolf 4 Seamus Heaney
5 The Water Babies

What does Santa teach the elves?

The elfabet

school notes

fun time

♥ Monday _____

_____

_____

♥ Tuesday _____

_____

_____

♥ Wednesday _____

_____

_____

♥ Thursday _____

_____

_____

♥ Friday _____

_____

it's the weekend

♥ Saturday

♥ Sunday

Brrrrrrr!

Emperor penguins are the biggest penguins at 120 centimetres in height. They live in Antarctica, where the temperature is -50 degrees Celsius – colder than a food deep-freezer.

Raining cats and frogs

1814, France – it started raining frogs during a thunderstorm.

1911, Indiana (US) – an alligator fell from the sky!

1894, Mississippi (US) – during a hailstorm a turtle in a block of ice fell from the sky.

1876, Kentucky (US) – lumps of raw meat fell from the sky, ugh!

1877, Tennessee (US) – a shower of snakes fell from the sky.

1968, Mexico – during a storm hundreds of maggots rained down.

QUIZ

1 The musical **Kiss Me Kate** was based on which Shakespeare play?

2 Which song did Survivor record as the theme for **Rocky III**?

3 Donald, Barlow, Williams, Owen and Orange are the surnames of which 90s boy band?

4 **Definitely Maybe** was the debut album of which group?

5 What is the stage name of the rap artist Sean Coombs?

answers
1 The Taming of the Shrew
2 'Eye Of The Tiger' 3 Take That
4 Oasis 5 P Diddy

Why were the dark ages so called?

Because there were so many knights!

month

school notes

fun time

Monday _____
_____
_____
_____

Tuesday _____
_____
_____
_____

Wednesday _____
_____
_____
_____

Thursday _____
_____
_____
_____

Friday _____
_____
_____

it's the weekend

Saturday
_____
_____
_____
_____

Sunday

Alien voice

Bob van der Houven is the voice of the alien dog, Stitch, in Disney's **Lilo and Stitch**. The unique voice was too difficult to dub into other languages, so Van der Houven voiced Stitch in the Dutch, German, Flemish and Italian versions of the film.

20th century discovery

1901 okapi
1901 Rothschild's giraffe
1902 mountain gorilla
1910 hero shrew
1913 pygmy hippo
1917 scaly-tailed possum
1926 Longman's beaked whale
1928 pygmy chimpanzee
1955 golden langur
1992 black-faced lion tamarin

QUIZ

1 The Wolsey in Ipswich and The Whitworth in Manchester are names of what?

2 In which US state is Anaheim, the home of a Disney theme park?

3 Capitoline Hill is the tallest hill in which European capital city?

4 Which English county is sometimes referred to as Constable Country?

5 The Althing is the parliament of which European country?

answers
1 Art galleries 2 California 3 Rome 4 Suffolk 5 Iceland

where do polar bears vote?

The North Poll

school notes

fun time

Monday _____

_____

_____

Tuesday _____

_____

Wednesday _____

_____

Thursday _____

_____

Friday _____

_____

it's the weekend

Saturday _____

Sunday _____

Green greed

Horses are fussy eaters. They have small stomachs and so need to eat little and often. A grazing horse takes 30,000 bites of grass in one day!

Birthdays in December

2 Britney Spears 1981
2 Lucy Liu 1968
3 Ozzy Osbourne 1948
4 Jay-Z 1970
8 Teri Hatcher 1964
14 Michael Owen 1979
18 Christina Aguilera 1980
18 Katie Holmes 1978
25 Dido 1971
30 Tiger Woods 1975

QUIZ

1 Which British royal family member founded a production company called Ardent Productions?

2 Who plays Gilderoy Lockhart in **Harry Potter and the Chamber Of Secrets**?

3 In the 2003 comedy **Bruce Almighty**, which actor played the role of God?

4 Which characters get married in the film **American Wedding**?

5 For which Bond film did Shirley Bassey sing the theme tune in 1971?

answers
1 Prince Edward 2 Kenneth Branagh 3 Morgan Freeman 4 Michelle and Jim 5 Diamonds Are Forever

Why do seagulls fly over the sea?

Because if they flew over the bay they would be bagels

school notes

fun time

Monday

Tuesday

Wednesday

Thursday

Friday

it's the weekend

Saturday

Sunday

Puppy power

A new puppy settles quickly into a home where preparations have been made for its arrival. At first, it should be kept in one room, with a bed provided. This can be a cardboard box, lined with old towels or jumpers to keep it warm.

super sea facts

The total salt in the world's seas would cover Europe in a layer 5 kilometres thick.

The Mariana trench in the Pacific is deep enough to fit 28 Empire State Buildings on top of each other.

There is more gold dissolved in the Earth's seawater than can be found on land.

The highest ever wave was 34 metres from trough to crest. Surf that!

Dolphins only ever sleep with half their brain at any time, to keep them alert to danger.

QUIZ

1 What makes the humming sound of the a hummingbird?

2 How many toes has an ostrich on each foot?

3 Welsh Mountain and Shetland are both breeds of what?

4 Which has the drier skin, a frog or a toad?

5 Whooper, trumpeter and mute are species of which bird?

1 The beating of its wings 2 Two 3 Pony 4 Toad 5 Swan

ANSWERS

What dog keeps the best time?

A watch dog

school notes

fun time

Monday _____
_____
_____

Tuesday _____
_____
_____

Wednesday _____
_____
_____

Thursday _____
_____
_____

Friday _____
_____
_____

it's the weekend

Saturday

Sunday

Meat munch

The hamburger is named after the German city of Hamburg, where a dish of fried minced beef was popular in the 1890s. Emigrants took the recipe with them to the United States, where a burger in a bun soon became a worldwide favourite.

Celeb initials

A A Milne (Alan Alexander Milne)

TPT (Tara Palmer Tomkinson)

Jay-Z (Shawn Carter)

J K Rowling (Joanne Kathleen Rowling)

CZJ (Catherine Zeta Jones)

JK (Jason Kay)

JFK (John Fitzgerald Kennedy)

LL Cool J (James Todd Smith – the initials stand for Ladies Love Cool James!)

J R R Tolkien (John Ronald Reuel Tolkien)

QUIZ

1 Which of the children's TV faves, the Teletubbies, is yellow?

2 Which number is opposite to four on a dice?

3 Which playing card is known as the black lady?

4 Gracie Mansion is the official residence of the mayor of which US city?

5 Which bird is shown on the Egyptian flag?

answers
1 La La 2 Three 3 Queen of Spades 4 New York 5 Eagle

Why did the tomato turn red?

It saw the salad dressing!

school notes

fun time

Monday

Tuesday

Wednesday

Thursday

Friday

it's the weekend

Saturday

Sunday

Sea schools

Common dolphins swim in schools of up to 3000. They are very acrobatic when swimming and their movement in the water can often make the sea look like it is boiling!

Basic body bits

patella – kneecap
mandible – jawbone
carpals – wristbones
femur – thigh bone
phalanges – toes
cranium – skull
scapula – shoulder blade
clavicle – collar bone
sternum – breastbone
tibia – shin bone

QUIZ

1 Which British prime minister was known as The Welsh Wizard?

2 Whose portrait features on the front of a US $100 bill?

3 Eisenhower, Kennedy, Johnson, Nixon – who came next?

4 Which German chancellor was voted into office in 1998?

5 In which year was Prince Charles born?

answers
1 David Lloyd George 2 Benjamin Franklin 3 Ford 4 Gerhard Schroeder 5 1948

What did the crushed grape do?

It let out a little wine!

school notes

fun time

❤ Monday _____
_____
_____
_____

❤ Tuesday _____
_____
_____
_____

❤ Wednesday _____
_____
_____
_____

❤ Thursday _____
_____
_____
_____

❤ Friday _____
_____
_____

it's the weekend

❤ Saturday _____
_____
_____
_____

❤ Sunday _____
_____
_____
_____

Secrets

Frances Hodgson Burnett published **The Secret Garden** in 1911. The story tells of a spoiled orphaned girl, Mary, who has to live with her uncle in England. Mary discovers a secret garden that had been hidden and locked away since the death of her aunt ten years previously.

Famous soccer fans

Robbie Williams – **Port Vale**
Ant and Dec – **Newcastle United**
Steve Coogan – **Man United**
Liam and Noel Gallagher – **Manchester City**
Holly Valance – **Southampton**
Dido – **Arsenal**
Damon Albarn – **Chelsea**
Peter Kay – **Bolton Wanderers**
Paul McCartney – **Everton**
Cat Deeley – **West Bromich Albion**

QUIZ

1 What word means *two* in the German language?

2 From which card game did *the* term Grand Slam originate?

3 Are *the* leather seats in *the* House of Commons red or green?

4 In which TV show did *the* character Kermit *the* frog first appear?

5 "Elliot" was *the* first spoken word of which extraterrestrial character?

answers
1 Zwei 2 Bridge 3 Green 4 Sesame Street 5 E.T.

What happens when an egg laughs?

It cracks up

school notes

fun time

Monday _____

_____

_____

Tuesday _____

_____

_____

Wednesday _____

_____

_____

Thursday _____

_____

_____

Friday _____

_____

_____

it's the weekend

Saturday _____

_____

_____

_____

_____

Sunday _____

_____

_____

_____

_____

City chimes

'Big Ben' doesn't actually refer to the clock tower, but to the huge 13-tonne bell. Since the 1850s, the bell has been replaced many times because it cracks under the constant hammering.

Celeb endorsements

Kate Moss – Burberry fashion
Cat Deeley – Shape spring water
Christina Aguilera – Skechers trainers
Helena Christensen – Imedeen fake tan
Liv Tyler – Givenchy perfume
Maria Sharapova – Tag Heuer watches
Claudia Schiffer – L'Oreal shampoo
Tara Palmer Tomkinson – Walkers Sensations crisps
Sara Jessica Parker – Lux shower gel
Beyoncé – L'Oreal hair cream

QUIZ

Can you identify these famous artists from these paintings?

From left to right: 1 Michelangelo 2 Renoir 3 Monet 4 Van Gogh

What did the judge say to the skunk?

Odour in the court

school notes

fun time

♥ Monday _____
_____
_____
_____

♥ Tuesday _____
_____
_____
_____

♥ Wednesday _____
_____
_____
_____

♥ Thursday _____
_____
_____
_____

♥ Friday _____
_____
_____

it's the weekend

♥ Saturday
_____
_____
_____

♥ Sunday
_____
_____
_____

Playtime

Kittens play with almost anything that moves. They are practising their hunting skills for when they get older.

Birthday in July

1 Missy Elliott 1971
3 Tom Cruise 1962
6 50 Cent 1976
10 Jessica Simpson 1980
17 David Hasselhof 1952
21 Josh Hartnett 1978
23 Daniel Radcliffe 1989
24 J-Lo 1970
25 Matt LeBlanc 1967
31 J K Rowling 1965

QUIZ

1 By which name is the fictional character of Don Diego de la Vega better known?

2 Which film saw Dustin Hoffman and Tom Cruise gambling in Las Vegas?

3 Who, according to Shakespeare, was the Queen of the Fairies?

4 In 1989, which electronics company bought Columbia Pictures?

5 Which Jane Austen novel was made into a film in 2005?

answers
1 Zorro 2 Rain Man 3 Titania
4 Sony 5 Pride & Prejudice

What did the water say to the boat?

Nothing, it just waved

school notes

fun time

♥ Monday _____

_____

_____

_____

♥ Tuesday _____

_____

_____

_____

♥ Wednesday _____

_____

_____

_____

♥ Thursday _____

_____

_____

_____

♥ Friday _____

_____

_____

it's the weekend

♥ Saturday

♥ Sunday

Crazy colour

Rainbows form when sunlight passes through raindrops, causing it to bend and split into the colours of the spectrum that make up light – violet, indigo, blue, green, yellow, orange and red. Most rainbows only last a few minutes, but one once lasted for six hours!

Money Money Money

The ancient Egyptians used shells as a form of currency.

Other ancient currencies included cocoa beans and feathers.

The ancient Greeks put a silver coin into a dead person's mouth to pay for the transportation of their soul.

Paper money was invented by the Chinese in the 10th century.

The first piggy banks existed in the 14th century.

Every day, 38 million US bills are printed to replace old ones.

QUIZ

1 In which country is the highest waterfall in the world?

2 The Bahamas lie off the coast of which US state?

3 Which African country has the highest population?

4 From which country did Iceland achieve independence in 1944?

5 Mount Cook is the highest peak in which country?

answers
1 Venezuela 2 Florida 3 Nigeria
4 Denmark 5 New Zealand

Why was six afraid of seven?

Because seven eight nine!

school notes

fun time

Monday _____

_____

_____

_____

Tuesday _____

_____

_____

_____

Wednesday _____

_____

_____

_____

Thursday _____

_____

_____

_____

Friday _____

_____

_____

it's the weekend

Saturday _____

_____

_____

Sunday _____

_____

_____

Pet invasion

Hamsters originally came from Syria in 1930, where a mother hamster and her 12 young were found. They were brought to England in 1931 and since then have become well-loved pets!

World's coldest cities

Norilsk, Russia
Yakutusk, Russia
Ulan-Bator, Mongolia
Fairbanks, USA
Chita, Russia
Bratsk, Russia
Ulan-Ude, Russia
Angarsk, Russia
Irkutsk, Russia
Komsomolsk-na-Amure, Russia

QUIZ

1. The film **Clueless** starring Alicia Silverstone, was based on which Jane Austen novel?

2. What type of bird dug the grave in the nursery rhyme "Who Killed Cock Robin"?

3. Who wrote the popular novels, **Angels and Demons** and **The Da Vinci Code**?

4. Which famous novel has an opening chapter entitled **A Long Expected Party**?

5. Michael Henchard is the mayor of which fictional town?

answers
1 Emma 2 Owl 3 Dan Brown
4 Lord of the Rings 5 Casterbridge

What's in a teddy bear's house?

Furrniture!

school notes

fun time

Monday _____

_____

_____

Tuesday _____

_____

_____

Wednesday _____

_____

_____

Thursday _____

_____

_____

Friday _____

_____

it's the weekend

Saturday _____

Sunday _____

Glitzy gems

Diamond is the hardest substance in nature and is used in industry to make cutting and grinding tools. Cut diamonds sparkle so brilliantly that they make valuable gems. The British Imperial State crown has over 3000!

The meaning of colours

Red – passion
Yellow – cowardice
Green – jealousy
Blue – sorrow
White – purity
Black – mourning
Purple – royalty
Gold – wealth
Silver – technology
Pink – romance

QUIZ

1. The name of which sport is derived from the French word for a shepherd's crook?
2. At which sports stadium would you find the Jack Hobbs Gates?
3. In which sport do competitors use a tab, a bracer and a chest guard?
4. Who was the first British Formula One World Champion?
5. Which city hosted the 1980 Summer Olympics?

1 Hockey 2 The Oval 3 Archery 4 Mike Hawthorn 5 Moscow

Why did the jelly wobble?

Because it saw the milk shake!

school notes

fun time

Monday _____
_____
_____

Tuesday _____
_____

Wednesday _____
_____

Thursday _____
_____

Friday _____
_____

it's the weekend

Saturday

Sunday

Uni-horn

The long tusklike tooth of the narwhal was once sold as the 'real horn' of the mythical horse called the unicorn. The tusk is actually a very long left upper tooth that grows with a corkscrew pattern.

90s one hit wonders

Macarena – Los Del Rio
Who Let The Dogs Out – Baha Men
Groove Is In the Heart – Deee-Lite
Jump Around – House Of Pain
Mambo No. 5 – Lou Bega
Achy Breaky Heart – Billy Ray Cyrus
Bitch – Meredith Brooks
Blue (Da Ba Dee) – Eifel 65
How Bizarre – OMC
Tubthumping – Chumbawamba

QUIZ

1. How old was screen siren Marilyn Monroe when she died?
2. Who was the first boxer to defeat Muhammed Ali?
3. Eastenders star Martin Kemp was the bassist in which 80s New Romantic band?
4. How many Oscars® has the actor Russell Crowe won?
5. Who was Britain's first Prime Minister?

answers
1 36 years old 2 Joe Frazier
3 Spandau Ballet 4 One For Gladiator
5 Robert Walpole

What's a chicken in a shellsuit called?

An egg!

month

school notes

fun time

Monday

Tuesday

Wednesday

Thursday

Friday

it's the weekend

Saturday

Sunday

Dainty dance

Ballet was originally developed in the 1700s as a theatre show in France. Among the most famous ballet dancers were Rudolf Nureyev and Margot Fonteyn, who took 89 curtain calls for **Swan Lake**.

Birthday in August

6 Geri Halliwell 1972
7 Charlize Theron 1975
8 Roger Federer 1981
14 Halle Berry 1968
15 Ben Affleck 1972
16 Madonna 1958
19 Matthew Perry 1969
20 Fred Durst 1971
21 Kim Cattrall 1956
30 Cameron Diaz 1972

QUIZ

1 Which animal does Dawn French play in the film **The Lion, the Witch and the Wardrobe**?

2 In which US comedy show did Courtney Cox play super-clean Monica?

3 Which children's TV show celebrated its 40th anniversary in 1998?

4 What was the name of Rodney Trotter's wife in **Only Fools and Horses**?

5 Which actress played Brad Pitt's wife in the film **Seven**?

Answers
1 Beaver 2 Friends
3 Blue Peter 4 Cassandra
5 Gwyneth Paltrow

What is a fear of Santa called?

Claustrophobia

month

school notes

fun time

Monday _____

_____

_____

_____

Tuesday _____

_____

_____

Wednesday _____

_____

_____

Thursday _____

_____

_____

Friday _____

_____

it's the weekend

Saturday _____

_____

_____

_____

Sunday _____

_____

_____

_____

Phone a friend

Name:

Address:

Telephone:
@ Email :
Birthday:

Name:

Address:

Telephone:
@ Email :
Birthday:

Name:

Address:

Telephone:
@ Email :
Birthday:

Name:

Address:

Telephone:
@ Email :
Birthday:

Name:

Address:

Telephone:
@ Email :
Birthday:

Name:

Address:

Telephone:
@ Email :
Birthday:

Name:

Address:

Telephone:
@ Email :
Birthday:

Name:

Address:

Telephone:
@ Email :
Birthday:

Name:

Address:

Telephone:
@ Email :
Birthday:

Name:

Address:

Telephone:
@ Email :
Birthday:

Name:

Address:

Telephone:

Email :

Birthday:

Name:

Address:

Telephone:

Email :

Birthday:

Name:

Address:

Telephone:

Email :

Birthday:

Name:

Address:

Telephone:

Email :

Birthday:

Name:

Address:

Telephone:

Email :

Birthday:

Name:

Address:

Telephone:

Email :

Birthday:

Name:

Address:

Telephone:

Email :

Birthday:

Name:

Address:

Telephone:

Email :

Birthday:

Name:

Address:

Telephone:

Email :

Birthday:

Name:

Address:

Telephone:

Email :

Birthday:

First published by Bardfield Press in 2006

Bardfield Press is an imprint of
Miles Kelly Publishing Ltd
Bardfield Centre, Great Bardfield, Essex, CM7 4SL

2 4 6 8 10 9 7 5 3 1

Editorial Director: Belinda Gallagher

Art Director: Jo Brewer

Editor: Amanda Askew

Editorial Assistant: Bethanie Bourne

Cover Designer: Louisa Leitao

Additional Design: Clare Harris

Picture Researcher: Laura Faulder

Reprograhics: Mike Coupe, Stephan Davis

Production Manager: Elizabeth Brunwin

Copyright © Miles Kelly Publishing Ltd 2006

All rights reserved. No part of this publication may be stored
in a retrieval system, or transmitted by any means, electronic,
mechanical, photocopying, recording or otherwise, without the
prior permission of the copyright holder.

ISBN 1-84236-694-7

Printed in China

British Library Cataloguing-in-Publication Data
A catalogue record for this book is available from
the British Library

ACKNOWLEDGEMENTS

All artworks are from Miles Kelly Artwork Bank

The publishers would like to thank the following sources
for the use of their photographs:
www.pictorialpress.com – pages 26, 30, 32, 40, 44, 48, 56,
62, 66, 68, 70, 80, 88, 102, 108, 114, 124 (TR)
Sony Computer Entertainment – pages 32 (B), 66, 76, 100 (TL)

All other photographs from:
Corel digitalSTOCK digitalvision Hemera PhotoAlto PhotoDisc

www.mileskelly.net
info@mileskelly.net